*Lorraine J de la Hoyde*

Born in London on 14 February 1964. People and Planet focused since childhood. Currently working with the FWA, also completing a Foundation Degree in Counselling. I aspire to develop a project enterprise for homeless young people in the form of a therapeutic community and maintain my life's commitment to *giving something back*, in particular the basic concepts of love, compassion, understanding and respect for self, others and our planet.

*For Chiv and the Planet's children.*
*Absorb your minds with nature's gifts*
*of love, respect and understanding*
*for this world and each other.*

*May all your hopes and dreams come true.*

*Seek And You Shall Find*
*Your Angel*

*Seek And You Shall Find*
*Your Angel*

Lorraine J de la Hoyde

Illustrated by Cheryl de la Hoyde

ATHENA PRESS

LONDON

ISBN 10-digit: 1 84748 078 0
ISBN 13-digit: 978 1 84748 078 1

First Published 2008
ATHENA PRESS
Queen's House, 2 Holly Road
Twickenham TW1 4EG
United Kingdom

Printed for Athena Press

*Special thanks to John (in his memory), Ali, Tessa, Ruthanna, Adelle, Mags, Marion and Fish for supporting a dream to come true. Big love to my twin sister Cheryl for her artistic excellence.*

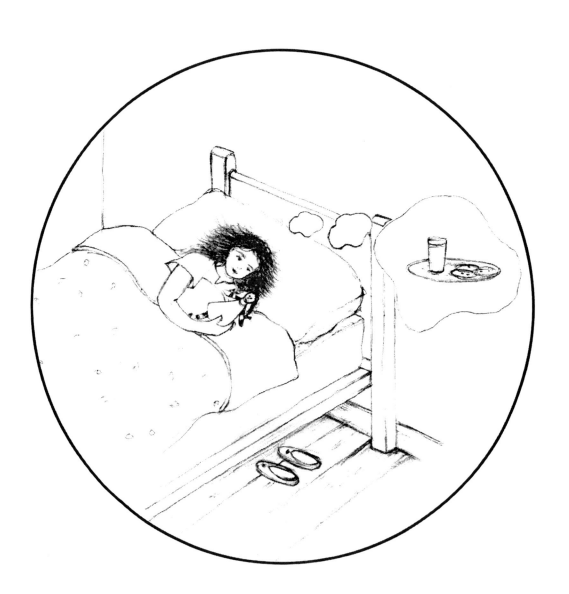

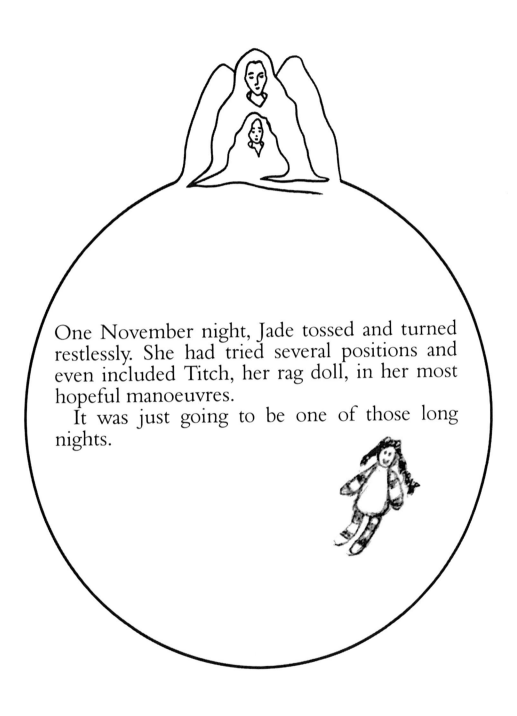

One November night, Jade tossed and turned
restlessly. She had tried several positions and
even included Titch, her rag doll, in her most
hopeful manoeuvres.

It was just going to be one of those long
nights.

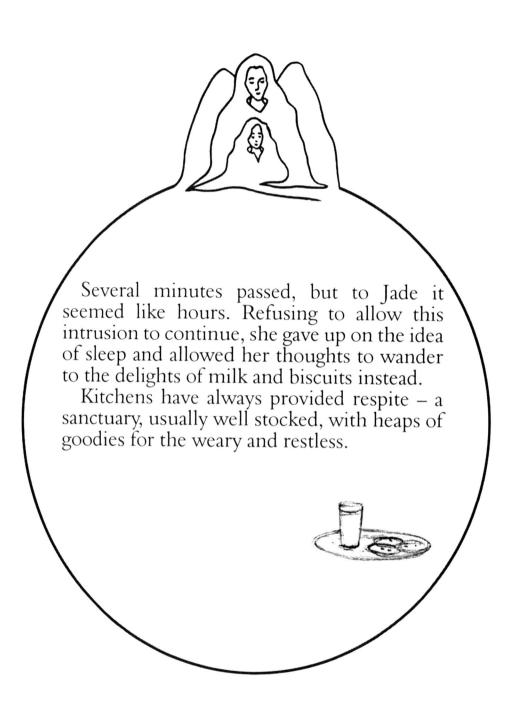

Several minutes passed, but to Jade it seemed like hours. Refusing to allow this intrusion to continue, she gave up on the idea of sleep and allowed her thoughts to wander to the delights of milk and biscuits instead.

Kitchens have always provided respite – a sanctuary, usually well stocked, with heaps of goodies for the weary and restless.

The mission would have to be a cautious one; approached with the lightness of an angel and using precise footwork to avoid the creaky boards.

The covers flew over to one side and Jade made a positive step towards her choice and intentions.

Aware that her inner excitement would overspill into erratic breathing, or even giggles, she held her breath tightly.

Poised like a ballerina ready to perform, she opened the door and, with the silence and grace of a tooth fairy, she made her getaway.

As her hand reached for the kitchen door handle, the mission was almost complete. But as light began to shine through the widening crack, shock and disbelief overcame Jade's mind as her mission was suddenly discovered.

A familiar, kindly voice said, 'Who's that? Jade, is that you?'

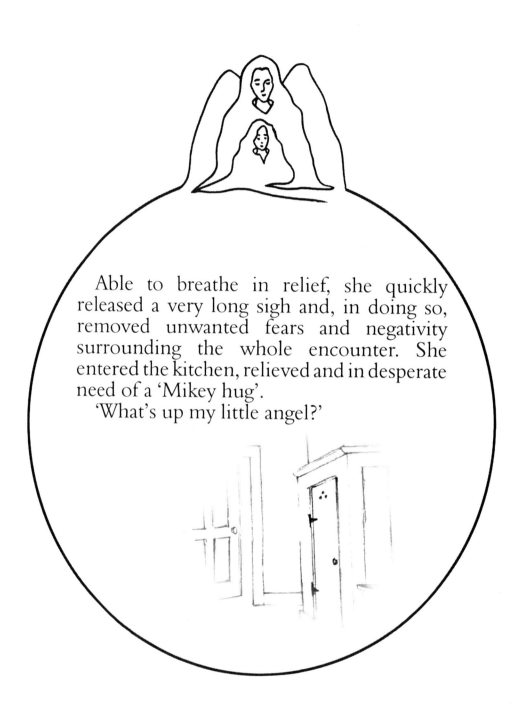

Able to breathe in relief, she quickly released a very long sigh and, in doing so, removed unwanted fears and negativity surrounding the whole encounter. She entered the kitchen, relieved and in desperate need of a 'Mikey hug'.

'What's up my little angel?'

Michael, approaching fourteen, was eight years older than Jade. He was the kindest, most loving and considerate elder brother you could ask for.

Already aware of his purpose in life, he had turned his back on many of the judgmental attitudes and self-centred trends associated with his peer group and, as a result, quite often found himself a target at school.

Michael had two like-minded friends whom he trusted and with whom he shared his innermost thoughts and experiences. He was a seeker of quality rather than quantity.

Eventually his peers would surely get bored of challenging his love and kindness and perhaps one day would try it as an alternative to fear.

'Come here,' he said with open arms, adjusting his legs to provide a seat of security, comfort and warmth for Jade. He guided her towards him and she leapt up and sat on his knee.

As her smile reached her eyes, Michael knew that Jade was, in this moment of time, happy and safe.

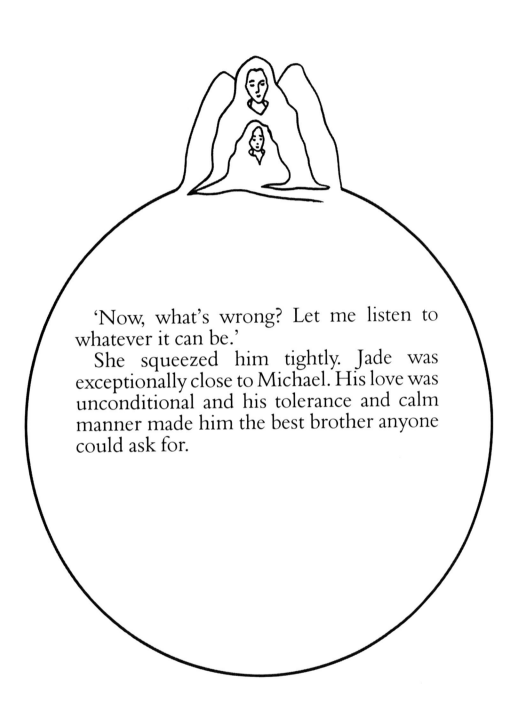

'Now, what's wrong? Let me listen to whatever it can be.'

She squeezed him tightly. Jade was exceptionally close to Michael. His love was unconditional and his tolerance and calm manner made him the best brother anyone could ask for.

She was also extremely grateful that it was him that was still up and not her mum.

'I can't sleep,' she replied, with her chocolate-button eyes looking up at him, designed to melt the sternest of hearts.

'So why don't you call for your dream angel?' suggested Michael.

'My dream angel? What's a dream angel?'

She envisaged a story time brewing and watched eagerly for his reaction.

'Let's find you a glass of milk and I'll tell you when you're tucked up in bed. OK?'

'OK,' she said without hesitation, and she jumped up and went to wait at the door.

'Walk up quietly because Mum's up really early tomorrow.'

Mum lived without Dad or any other partner. They had decided to go their own separate ways and move on with their lives. They had, however, remained true friends throughout and had a very positive and balanced method of parenting which was fully accepted by both children.

Jade nodded and held out her hand in readiness for their plan to materialise.

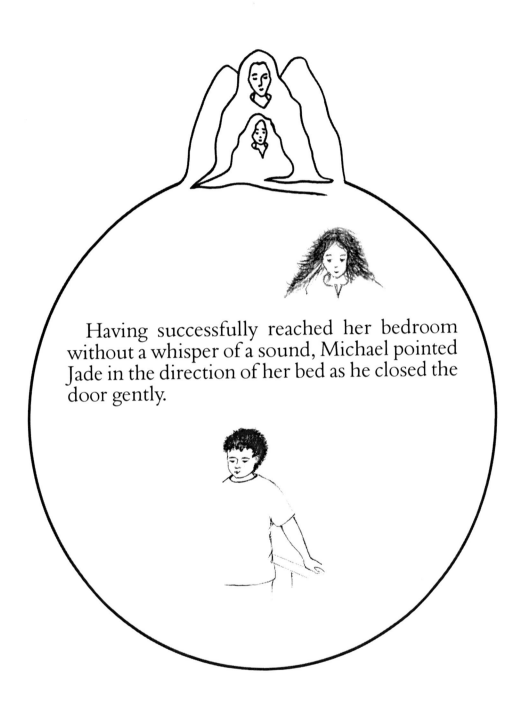

Having successfully reached her bedroom without a whisper of a sound, Michael pointed Jade in the direction of her bed as he closed the door gently.

Jade had settled snugly in bed, with Titch beside her head so that she could hear the story too.

'Ready?'

She nodded and puckered her lips and nose in anticipation.

'Close your eyes and I will begin,' instructed Michael.

'Now relax, breathe slowly and deeply, free your body and mind from all your worries.

'Imagine that you are in a beautiful place, surrounded by the sound, smell and peace of nature.

'Become part of it; sink your feet into the running stream and feel the water trickle delicately across your toes. Now feel that you truly are a part of nature and imagine that you have roots growing from your feet.

'In the background you can hear the water flowing to its own music, and the birds singing so sweetly that when you close your eyes all you can see is the whiteness and brightness of nature's unspoilt purity.

'When you have this light I will tell you about your angels; and, in particular, your dream angel.'

'I have the light. I have the light, Michael,' she replied. '*Angels*... you mean there's more than one type of angel?'

'Yes. *Shh* and I will tell you. Continue as you were before. Ready?'

He began.

'Angels surround us everywhere, anywhere and always. They are helpers, messengers and guardians for the whole universe. When you need their help, just ask and they will hear you calling.

'They are here to help us, guide us, protect us, love us and be close to us in times of fear and sadness. Angels are there for all occasions and for all living things. Some say they are "God's helpers".'

Jade did not comment. 'Everyone has an angel – even you. A whisper from inside you; a sudden thought from nowhere; those tingly sensations and the warm, bright glow throughout your body – this is your dream angel. Like when you know you have done something that's right for you, and joy travels through your body bringing a smile to your inside and outside; that's your angel either sending you a message or saying, "I am here".

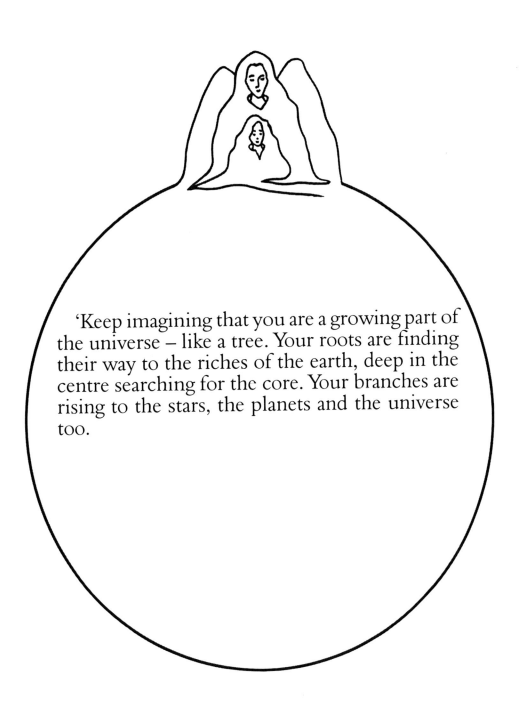

'Keep imagining that you are a growing part of
the universe – like a tree. Your roots are finding
their way to the riches of the earth, deep in the
centre searching for the core. Your branches are
rising to the stars, the planets and the universe
too.

'Breathe in the life from the earth and the light from the universe and let it fill you with its energy of love and joy. Then, ask your dream angel for peaceful and happy dreams.

'Are you doing what I say my little angel?' There was no response.

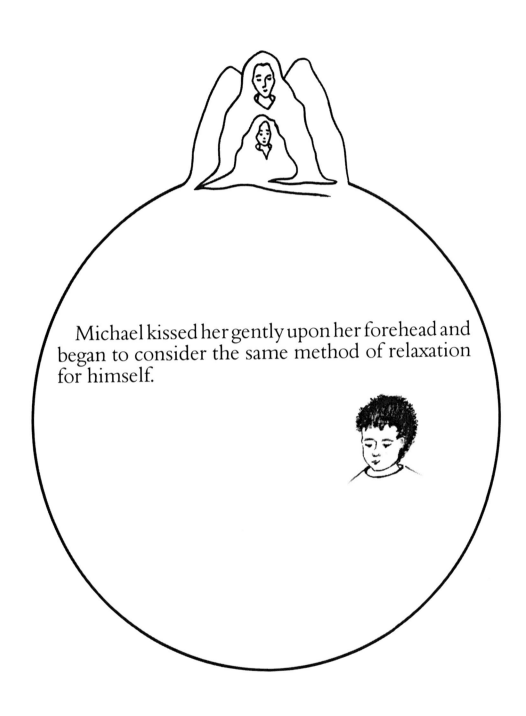

Michael kissed her gently upon her forehead and began to consider the same method of relaxation for himself.

Morning came and Jade awoke.

Grabbing Titch by the first available limb, she bolted downstairs to share her dream.

'Michael, Michael!

'Orielle took me by the hand! Orielle took me by the hand! She's my very own angel and she showed me other angels, even those that protect the kingdoms of the universe. The universe is bigger than we can dream; more beautiful than the sunshine. Michael, Michael, I have my very own angel.'

Michael took Jade's tiny hands, initially to stop her from jumping up and down and also to let her know that he was listening to her joy and hoping she would soon remember to take a breath.

He placed her on a chair and replied, 'Tell me, slowly.' He released her hands, as they would surely be used continuously during the description of her dream.

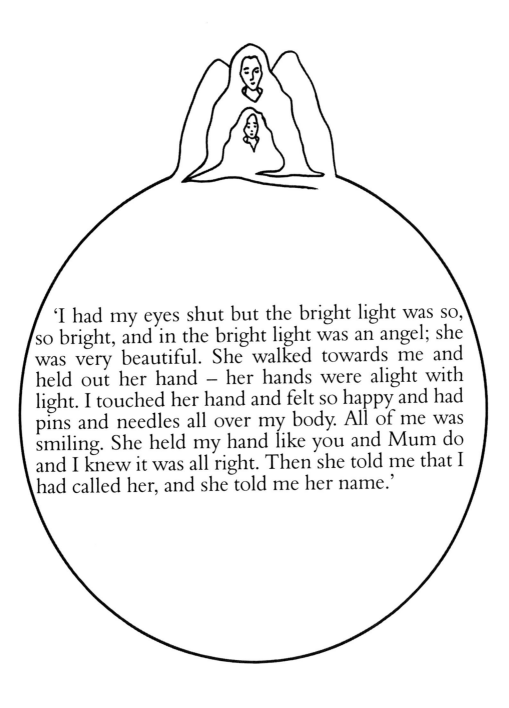

'I had my eyes shut but the bright light was so, so bright, and in the bright light was an angel; she was very beautiful. She walked towards me and held out her hand – her hands were alight with light. I touched her hand and felt so happy and had pins and needles all over my body. All of me was smiling. She held my hand like you and Mum do and I knew it was all right. Then she told me that I had called her, and she told me her name.'

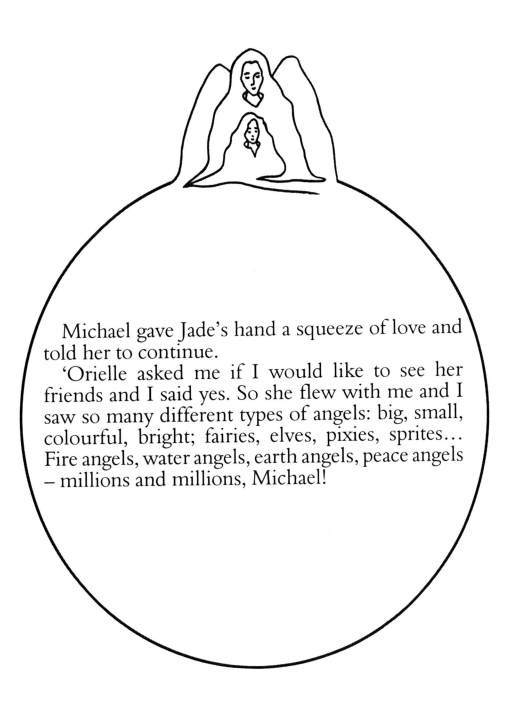

Michael gave Jade's hand a squeeze of love and told her to continue.

'Orielle asked me if I would like to see her friends and I said yes. So she flew with me and I saw so many different types of angels: big, small, colourful, bright; fairies, elves, pixies, sprites… Fire angels, water angels, earth angels, peace angels – millions and millions, Michael!

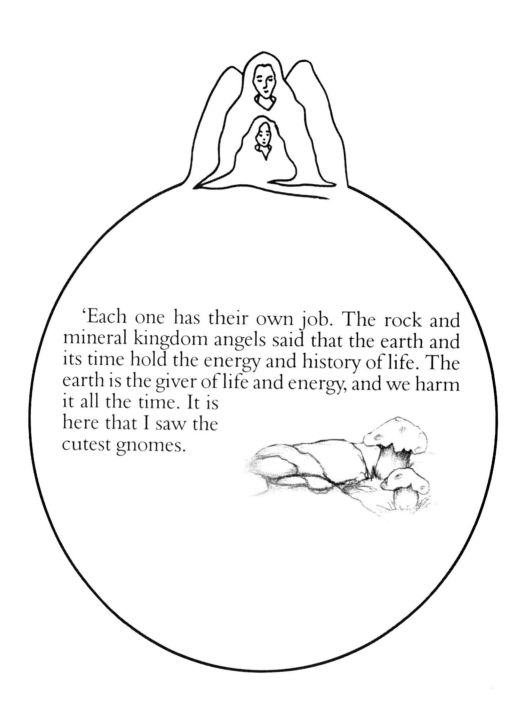

'Each one has their own job. The rock and mineral kingdom angels said that the earth and its time hold the energy and history of life. The earth is the giver of life and energy, and we harm it all the time. It is here that I saw the cutest gnomes.

'The crystal kingdom angels were full of life and colours within colours. They stay close to the ground and feed it with life, goodness, love, light and energy. Without this kingdom there would be no plants. Without plants – no animals, and no us.

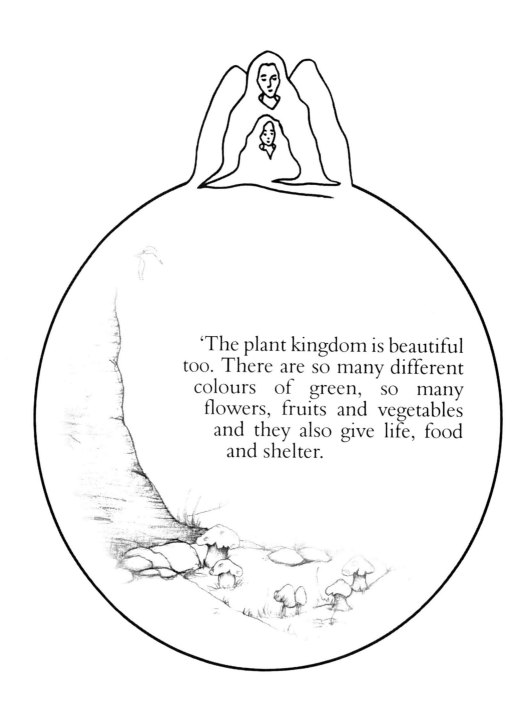

'The plant kingdom is beautiful too. There are so many different colours of green, so many flowers, fruits and vegetables and they also give life, food and shelter.

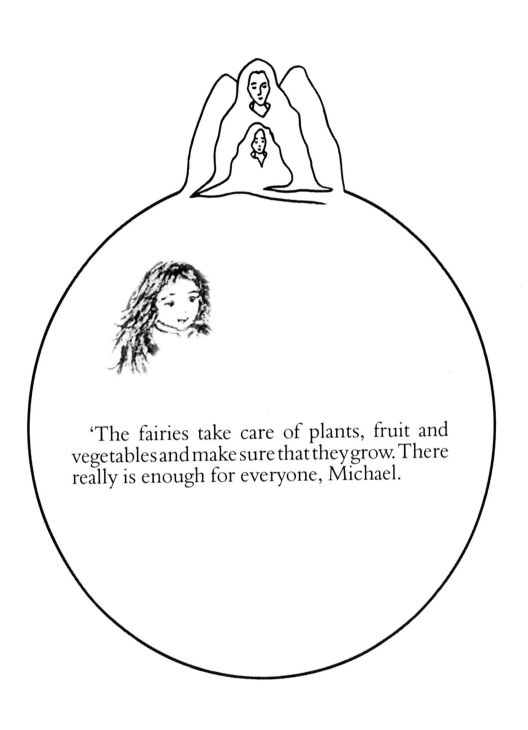

'The fairies take care of plants, fruit and vegetables and make sure that they grow. There really is enough for everyone, Michael.

'The animals don't hate each other, they respect each other and do what they *know* instead of what they *think* and that's why they can live more peacefully than we do – they only take what they need.

'The angels respect and care for the universe, even the air. Why can't we?

'I think our planet is very pretty and when I grow up I'm going to love it and help the angels of all the kingdoms. I know we are all one.'

She stopped and looked into Michael's eyes, or was it his soul? He was speechless.

'Why didn't you tell me about angels before?' she asked enquiringly.

'Judging by your inner joy and fulfilment, I think my timing was just right, my little angel.' He tussled her hair and gave her a soul-felt 'Mikey hug'.

She smiled an everlasting smile, for what she had experienced had truly taught her the meaning and purpose of life.

Printed in the United Kingdom
by Lightning Source UK Ltd.
127484UK00001B/17-48/P